Contents

The **Mermaids** of the

Molly

Ella

Delphi

Shivana

The Secret Mermaid

Deep Trouble

Sue Mongredien

Illustrated by Maria Pearson

USBORNE

For Ella, Darcey and Marnie Howe,
with lots of love

First published in the UK in 2009 by Usborne Publishing Ltd., Usborne House,
83-85 Saffron Hill, London EC1N 8RT, England. www.usborne.com

Text copyright © Sue Mongredien Ltd., 2009
Illustration copyright © Usborne Publishing Ltd., 2009

A CIP catalogue record for this book is available from the British Library.

JFMAMJJA OND/17   01526/7

ISBN 9780746096185

Printed in India.

Undersea Kingdom

Coral

Queen Luna

Princess Silva

Pearl

Chapter One

Dear Katie,

How are you? It feels like ages since we said goodbye. What have you been up to without me? Have you got a new best friend now?

Things are pretty good in Horseshoe Bay. I miss you and everyone else from school, but I do really like living by the sea in Gran's house. And, Katie, you just wouldn't BELIEVE some of the things that have happened to me here...

Molly Holmes wrinkled her nose and put
her pen down. No, she shouldn't have written
that bit. Much as she was dying to tell her

friend about her adventures, she knew she wasn't allowed. Besides, Katie would only think she was making up stories if Molly told her she'd been magically turned into a mermaid, and how she'd made friends with the Shell-Keeper mermaids of the Undersea Kingdom...

Molly grinned to herself. It did sound far-fetched. If one of her friends had claimed such magical adventures had happened to *them*, Molly wouldn't have believed them either. But in this case, it was actually true! Since Molly and her family had moved here to live with Gran, Molly had become a secret mermaid at night-time – four times now! – and was helping her new mermaid friends find their missing pieces of a magical shell.

And hopefully I can help them find the last two pieces soon, Molly thought to herself, gazing out of her bedroom window at the sea below. Molly's dad had set up her desk in front of the window so that she could sit and draw pictures, or write letters to her old friends, with the most wonderful beach view. Just today, she and Mum had unpacked a box of Molly's stuff that included all her nicest pens and stationery, and her secret diary too. Oh, there was so much to write in *that*!

Molly looked out of the window again, cupping her chin in one hand. The sun was starting to sink in the sky now, turning a fiery orange and casting vivid reflections in the water below. On the beach, the last few visitors were folding deckchairs and shaking sand from their towels, preparing to go home. Up in the sky, seagulls soared high, shrieking to one another.

There was a knock at the bedroom door just then and Molly turned to see her mum standing in the doorway. "Nearly time to think about bed," Mrs. Holmes said. "Would you pop down and say goodnight to your gran? I think her leg's hurting, so it would save her having to climb the stairs."

"Sure," Molly said, stuffing her half-written letter into the desk drawer. She'd start a new one to Katie tomorrow, she vowed – and next time, she'd have to try harder not to hint at any of her mermaid adventures!

She followed her mum downstairs to where Gran was sitting in the living room, her feet up on a stool as she watched the television. "Goodnight, Gran," Molly said, sitting down on the sofa next to the elderly lady and snuggling into her side.

"Goodnight, Molly dear." Gran put her arms around Molly and held her close for a few moments, her woolly cardigan tickling Molly's bare arms.

Then there was a muffled *boom!* from the television and Molly jumped. "What was that?" she asked, staring at the screen. There was some sort of underwater scene, with what appeared to be great plumes of smoke billowing up from a rocky surface.

Molly's dad, who had been reading the newspaper in the armchair, looked up too. "Goodness! What's going on?" he asked.

"It's a deep-sea volcanic eruption," Gran replied. "There have been lots recently – the scientists can't explain it."

Molly was still transfixed by the image on the screen – the clouds of smoke pouring through the water. "I didn't think you could *have* smoke underwater?" she asked in confusion. "I mean – smoke comes from fire, doesn't it, so..." Her voice trailed away as she struggled with the idea of a fire burning at the bottom of the ocean.

"Ahh, but think of the earth beneath the sea," her dad said. "You know what causes a volcano on land, don't you?"

"Um..." Molly tried to think back to what she'd learned about volcanoes at school, but her mind was a blank.

"Well, it's when there's a rupture or crack in the earth's surface which allows very hot gas and molten rock – or lava – to escape," her dad said.

"And it's the same for areas under the sea."

Molly frowned. "What, so you get lava coming out into the sea?" she asked.

Her dad nodded. "That's right," he said. "And because the sea cools the lava very quickly, it forms strange rocky shapes in the water. I think they're called chimneys. Sometimes, if there's lots and lots of lava, it can even form new islands."

"Wow," Molly said, taking it in. On the television, she could now see tall, steep pillars of rock looming on the seabed, like strange ghostly buildings.

"There," her dad said, pointing at the rocky pillars. "Those are the chimneys I was telling you about."

The lava chimneys did look odd, Molly thought. Mind you, she'd recently discovered all sorts of weird and wonderful things about

the ocean. Not only were there the most
beautiful plants and creatures she'd ever seen,
there were the mermaids, too – including her
new friends, the Shell-Keepers, but also their
enemy, the evil Dark Queen Carlotta...

Molly shivered, not wanting to think about Carlotta. She hadn't met the Dark Queen herself before, but had fought off several of her followers. They had been scary enough for Molly!

Gran had noticed Molly's shiver. "Are you cold, poppet?" she asked in surprise.

Molly shook her head. "No," she said, "just...thinking about something." She risked a glance up at her grandmother's face, and the look of understanding in the elderly lady's eyes told Molly she needn't say any more. For Gran was the only other person who knew about the mermaids, of course. Long ago, Gran had been a secret mermaid herself, before giving Molly the magical shell which had taken her into the mermaid world in the first place.

Molly cuddled her gran one last time. "I'd better go to bed," she said, and went over to hug her dad. "Goodnight."

"Sleep well, honey," her dad said, kissing her nose.

"Sweet dreams," Gran said, with a meaningful look.

Molly felt apprehensive as she went up the stairs to her bedroom. She couldn't help wondering if the eruptions of the deep-sea volcanoes she'd just seen on the television had anything to do with the fact that two pieces of the Shell-Keeper mermaids' magical conch were still missing somewhere in the ocean... How she hoped her own shell would work its amazing magic again soon so that she could find out.

Once her mum had said goodnight and left the room in darkness, Molly picked up her special shell from where she kept it on the bedside table. It had been threaded onto a silver chain so that it could be worn as a necklace, and she held it up, letting it swing gently in front of her. "Please let me be a mermaid again tonight," she whispered into the warm evening air. "I think my friends need help. Please!"

Chapter Two

Still holding her shell, Molly shifted into a more comfortable position on her side and closed her eyes...then immediately felt as if she were falling through the air. Down, down, down...

Her heart raced – she knew that this meant her shell was working its magic again! She could feel her legs tingle, and then that strange melting sensation came over them, as if they were dissolving. And now she could feel cool water against her skin as she fell deeper and deeper, her eyes still closed...

She slowed to a halt and opened her eyes. She was a mermaid again – yes, there was her beautiful tail sparkling behind her! – and she was down in the ocean once more, wearing a turquoise top and her conch necklace. But something felt wrong.

She jumped in alarm as a loud rumbling noise started up and the ground shuddered below her.

The seabed was shaking! She stared around, noticing that the water was completely empty of sea creatures. Where had they all gone? What was happening?

The ground became still after a few seconds and the rumbling died away. Thank goodness! Molly's pulse slowed as she gazed about tentatively. She was in very deep water, she could tell – it felt much cooler and seemed darker and gloomier than the other parts of the ocean she'd explored.

She tipped her head back and stared above her – then felt dizzy as she realized just how far up the surface was. Not that she needed air to breathe now, of course. As a mermaid she could breathe underwater, but all the same, it was rather unnerving to think just how deep the water was – and how she was all the way down at the bottom of it.

It was a relief to hear a friendly voice calling her name at that moment. "Molly! Molly! I'm over here!"

Molly turned gratefully to see another mermaid swimming towards her. "Pearl!" she said, recognizing her at once. Pearl was one of the five other Shell-Keeper mermaids and she looked after the deepest parts of the ocean with the help of her magical conch piece.

Pearl had long brown
hair which she wore in
bunches tied with green ribbons, big
brown eyes and a shy smile. "I'm so glad to
see you," Molly said as Pearl drew closer.
"I heard this rumbling – and the ground
seemed to be shaking and..."

Pearl nodded, not smiling any more. "It's one of the volcanoes," she said. "My piece of the conch can usually keep them from erupting too often, but since it's been missing, the volcanoes are beyond my control. So many eruptions mean areas of water have become very sooty, and many fish have died." She sighed miserably. "I just wish I could find my conch piece!"

Molly knew that there were six pieces of the magical conch shell in all. As the secret

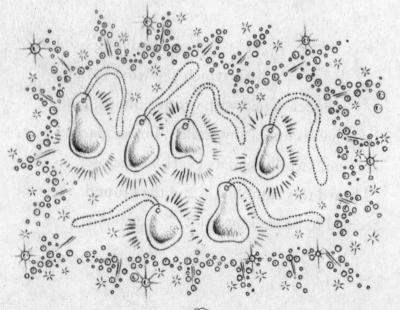

mermaid, she had one of them, and the Shell-Keepers looked after the remaining five – or at least they had until Carlotta, the Dark Queen, had stolen them. Carlotta had hidden them in her cave, but when Molly first arrived in the Undersea Kingdom, a burst of mermaid magic had sent those stolen pieces of shell spinning out into the ocean. Nobody knew where they were – and Carlotta was just as desperate to get them back as the Shell-Keeper mermaids were. She wanted to use the shell's power for her own wicked plans, and Molly knew that her army of followers had been patrolling the seas, searching out the shell pieces on her orders.

Luckily, Molly had already helped Coral, Ella and Delphi, three of the Shell-Keepers, to find their pieces of the shell. But two pieces were yet to be found.

Molly was just about to reply
to Pearl when she saw a bright
light approaching through the
gloomy water...followed by one
of the most peculiar-looking
creatures she'd ever seen.
It was a round, brown fish, a little
smaller than a netball, with staring eyes,
a huge mouth, and scarily sharp lower
teeth. The strangest thing of all was
that the creature had a spike
sticking straight out of its head
with a glowing light on
the end.

Molly stifled a scream and grabbed her friend's hand. "Pearl," she said, her voice trembling. "What's that?"

Pearl turned – and then smiled. "It's an anglerfish," she said. "Not one of nature's prettiest creations, is she?"

The anglerfish was swimming purposefully towards them, but before it could reach the two mermaids, the rumbling noise started up again. The anglerfish seemed frightened by the sound and darted away, its light bobbing up and down as it went.

The rumbling made Molly feel nervous too. "Is that the volcano again?" she asked.

Pearl nodded, her eyes wide and anxious. "It's coming from over there," she said, pointing to what seemed to be a large rocky hillock about ten metres away. Black smoke spurted alarmingly from a hole in the top.

"Quick, Molly. We need to go – right now!"

Pearl grabbed Molly's hand and the pair of them swam swiftly away, surging through the water at top speed.

BOOM! A huge explosion sounded behind the mermaids and the water became clouded with smoke. Molly glanced back and could see boiling water shooting out of the top of the volcano, spraying horribly close to them. The temperature was rising in the water. They would be scalded if they didn't get safely away in time!

"Keep going!" Pearl shouted, still holding Molly's hand.

Molly was glad of Pearl's fingers around her own because smoke was pouring down all about them now, making the sea darker and gloomier than ever. The ground was shaking and rumbling below, churning up the water as if it were being stirred about by a giant hand. Molly swam on blindly, feeling very scared, and wishing she and Pearl were far, far away from the deep-sea volcanoes. She didn't like it down here at all!

After a few moments, the rumbling grumbled away to nothing, and the smoke began to clear. The water became cooler once more and the mermaids stopped by a cluster of rocks to catch their breath.

Molly felt her heartbeat subside to its normal pace. "We really need to find your shell," she said. "I don't feel very safe down here, with volcanoes going off. It's scary!"

"I agree," Pearl said.

"The deep is a lonely place at the best of times and it feels even more deserted now. Many of the creatures are too wary to swim in these waters while the volcanoes are active. It's dangerous for them to be here – they instinctively stay away."

"Well, *there's* someone who's still hanging around," Molly said in a low voice, pointing to her left. "Here comes the anglerfish again – with a few friends this time."

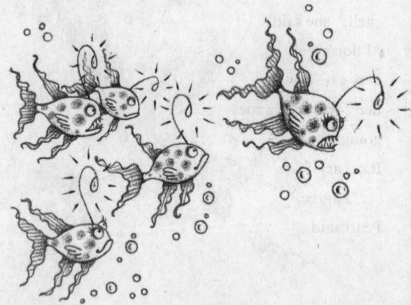

Pearl and Molly watched as five or six anglerfish swam towards them, their lights bobbing in front of their faces. They reminded Molly of coal miners' helmets with torches on the front, shining through the darkness.

The lead anglerfish clashed her teeth together excitedly as she drew closer to the mermaids, and Molly found herself backing away, unnerved. The fish's teeth were *very* sharp – and she had such an enormous mouth.

"There are strangers in the deep!" the anglerfish told Pearl, her teeth making rasping noises against each other. Her light flashed on and off as she spoke. "Bad strangers. Sea snakes from the Dark Queen. We have seen them!"

Molly felt a lurch inside at the words. Sea snakes? She didn't like snakes on land, let alone ones that could swim through the sea. And if they were loyal to the Dark Queen, they were sure to be up to no good here...

Pearl looked unnerved at the news too. "Really? Where did you see them?" she asked.

"They are circling Crater Mountain," the anglerfish replied. "Many, many snakes have gathered there."

"Crater Mountain?" Pearl repeated, frowning. "I wonder why?"

"We know why," a second anglerfish said in a low, wheezy voice. "Because your shell is

there, mermaid. We have
seen it shining.
We came to tell
you that we
found it."

"You
found my
shell? Oh,
wow!" Pearl
somersaulted
through the
water in
excitement. "But…
wait! You mean the
snakes have found it too?"

The two anglerfish who'd been speaking
exchanged glances as if they were worried about
telling her. "Yes," said the first one, after a small
hesitation. "Although the snakes have not yet

taken it. The thing is…"

"It's not such good news as it seems," the second added.

Then, after another worried glance between them, they made the announcement together. "Your shell is inside Crater Mountain," they chorused.

The smile slipped from Pearl's face. "Oh no," she said, looking horrified. "*Inside?*"

Molly didn't understand. "Can't we just go in and get it out again?"

Pearl shook her head. Her face was pale. "Not exactly," she replied. "You see, Crater Mountain is a volcano. The biggest volcano in the ocean!"

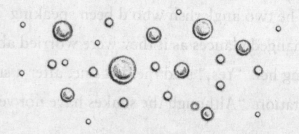

Chapter Three

Now Molly knew why her friend looked so scared. She didn't want to swim inside an active volcano either. But they really had to get Pearl's piece of the magic conch to safety, especially if the Dark Queen had already sent her sea snakes to hunt it out. It was a bit spooky the way the Dark Queen always seemed to know where the conch pieces were, Molly thought, biting her lip. It was as if she had spies everywhere.

The anglerfish made funny little bowing movements with their heads and swam away. "Thank you," Pearl called after them, adding to Molly in a low voice, "I think."

"I know what you mean," Molly said. She remembered the eruption they'd just escaped from, and how the boiling water had gushed out in great jets. Then an idea struck her. "Unless... well, maybe we don't have to actually swim *into* the volcano itself," she said slowly. "What if we wait for it to blow? It'll send your shell shooting right out the top, won't it?"

Pearl twisted her lips together uncertainly. "It might do," she agreed, "but then again, it might blast out red-hot lava. And what if my shell gets caught up in that?"

"Hmmm," said Molly. "I guess we'd better head to Crater Mountain and have a look. We have to stop the sea snakes from stealing your shell away."

Pearl nodded. "You're right," she said. "There's no other option. Let's go, before it's too late."

The two mermaids set off through the murky sea. The water became even deeper and darker, and Molly found herself wishing she had a light above her head to guide the way, like the anglerfish. They passed a mass of shadowy slithering creatures and Molly froze in fear for a second. "Don't worry," Pearl reassured her. "They're eels, not snakes."

Then they swam past the most enormous creature Molly had ever seen in her life – what looked like a pale gleaming *monster*, with masses of rubbery tentacles covered in suction cups, and colossal staring eyes.

"It's a giant squid," Pearl said, grabbing Molly's hand and pulling her along a little quicker. "They've always been nice to me in the past, but they are so huge, and such deadly hunters, that I can't help feeling a tiny bit nervous of them."

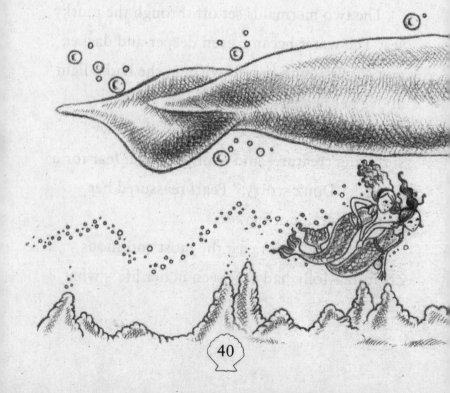

"Me too," Molly agreed with a shudder. The squid was longer than a bus and its tentacles looked soft but lethal. Swimming into a volcano would surely be less scary than wrestling with a giant squid, she thought to herself, and flicked her tail fin hard to send her even faster through the water.

A few minutes later, Pearl stopped in
front of a broad rocky mountain that
stretched from the seabed almost
up to the surface of the water
above. It was cone-shaped
and Molly could just
about see its wide,
flat top.

"Where are the snakes?" she wondered aloud. "Do you think the anglerfish got it wrong? Or…" She gulped as an awful thought struck her. "Or do you think they've already got your shell and gone?" Pearl turned pale. "I guess we'll have to swim up and look inside the volcano to find out," she replied.

Molly nodded and took a deep breath. Now that they'd arrived at Crater Mountain, she felt trembly at the idea of swimming down into it. She tried to hide those feelings, though. "Let's do it," she said. "The sooner the better."

Molly and Pearl swam up towards the top of the volcano. The water was eerily quiet and Molly kept glancing around nervously, expecting to see a snake swimming up behind them.

It took a couple of minutes to swim all the way up to the top of the steep volcano. The water seemed much lighter and clearer as they neared the surface of the sea. Once at the outer rim, Molly and Pearl peered down inside the crater to see that it looked like a hollow cavern. A cavern full of...

Molly gulped. "Oh my goodness," she said, feeling rather faint. "Have you *seen* all those snakes?"

There were masses of them, writhing inside the volcano in a sinister dark tangle. Their bodies were black and yellow, rippling through the water, their flat-ended tails acting like paddles to push them along. And they all had bright red eyes, just like every other creature the Dark Queen had enslaved into her army.

Molly shivered, backing away a little. How would it feel to have a snake's fangs biting down into your skin? she wondered.

"Have you seen what else is in there, though?" Pearl asked in a low voice. "Look past them, right down at the bottom – see it?"

Molly peered in again and there, further down inside, she caught a glimpse of magical sparkles, glimmering faintly beneath the mass of snakes. That had to be Pearl's shell, just as the anglerfish had said – so it was still there! That was good news...but how on earth were they going to get it?

"Why haven't the snakes already taken it?" she wondered.

"Maybe they're guarding it until the Dark Queen gets here," Pearl suggested. "We can't wait around for that, though. We've got to try and get it ourselves."

"Yes," Molly said reluctantly, not wanting to go anywhere near the snakes. The thought of them slithering against her skin made her feel sick.

"We'll have to be very careful," Pearl went on. "They're poisonous, so remember to ask your conch for help if you think one is about to strike."

"I will," said Molly, and her fingers stole impulsively around her shell, which dangled from its chain. Its magic had already helped her many times in the ocean and she was very glad to have it there with her for protection. She took a deep breath. "Let's get this over with, then."

Pearl led the way into the volcano, skimming

through the water and keeping close to the
volcano wall, well clear of the snakes.

Molly followed. "It's warm in here," she
commented. After the cooler waters of the deep,
it felt like slipping into a bath.

"Let's hope it doesn't get much warmer," Pearl said, rather more doubtfully.

To Molly's surprise, once she and Pearl were further down inside the volcano, she realized that the snakes weren't actually very close to the magical conch piece that lay at the bottom. The piece of shell was right by the inner wall of the volcano, at a safe distance from the red-hot lava that bubbled ominously in the centre of the volcano's floor. The snakes were swarming in a mass about five metres higher, their long muscular bodies thrashing and writhing so that they all looked part of the same black and yellow creature. Every now and then, one snake would dart lower towards the shell, its red eyes blazing, but then, just as quickly, it would rise away from it again, and rejoin the mass.

"It's too hot for them down there," Pearl worked out. "I think the heat must have dulled their senses – that's why they're not trying to attack us, Molly."

It *was* hot, Molly agreed. The water directly above the lava was actually boiling – churning with bubbles of hot gas. She knew she and Pearl would be horribly scalded if they had to swim right down to the shell.

"Do you think it's going to—?" she started, then broke off. She'd been about to ask if Pearl thought the volcano would erupt, but a great thundering noise started around them before she could finish her sentence.

Oh no. Molly felt a cold stab of terror at the sound, and her heart thumped inside her. Was the volcano really about to erupt, with her and Pearl still inside it? Surely they'd never survive *that*!

"We've got to get out of here," Pearl said, grabbing Molly. "Forget the shell. We've got to get out of here right now before Crater Mountain blows!"

Chapter Four

Molly hesitated, not moving. She couldn't drag
her eyes away from Pearl's shell down there at
the bottom of the volcano. It was so
tantalizingly close – the thought of having to
leave it behind was unbearable!

She grabbed her own conch piece, wondering
if its magical powers might be able to do
anything to stop the eruption. "Conch – calm
the volcano!" she cried, her voice sounding

small against the deafening rumblings.

Her shell glowed brightly for a few moments but nothing magical happened, and Molly felt dismay sink through her. Of course her shell was no match for the might of Crater Mountain!

"Hurry, Molly," Pearl said, tugging at her hand. "We've got to go, this second – the lava is rising, look!"

Pearl was right. The molten lava was higher at the bottom of the volcano now, bubbling like thick red soup. A boiling jet of water shot past them, its great hot bubbles missing them by just a few centimetres.

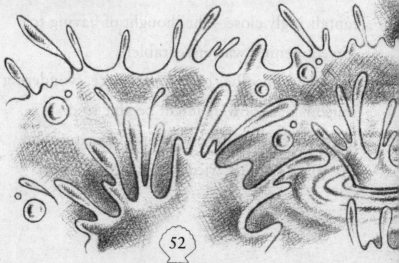

Molly clutched at her conch piece again, not wanting to leave Pearl's shell. "Conch, please help!" she cried desperately. "Keep us safe!"

Immediately, Molly's shell glowed a bright gold, and magical sparkles shot out from it. Molly held her breath as the sparkles whirled around her and Pearl. "What's happening?" she cried.

"I don't know," Pearl replied with a nervous glance down at the lava. The magical sparkles went on shooting out from Molly's shell, weaving a glittery gold-tinged...*bubble* all around them. Then, with a dazzling flash of golden light, the bubble sealed, and everything went silent.

Molly's mouth fell open in surprise. Her shell had created this bubble for them...but was it really enough to protect them from the volcano? She prodded the bubble wall tentatively. It was springy and soft, like being in a watery golden cobweb. "It's keeping out the heat," she realized in delight. "Oh my goodness! This is perfect. We can go deeper now – we can swim down and get your conch!"

"Let's try," Pearl said eagerly. "As fast as we can!"

Molly and Pearl pushed the bubble forwards
with their hands, sending it further into the
rumbling volcano. To their amazement, they felt
perfectly cool inside it, even though they
were near the bottom now.

"There's the shell!" Pearl cried, pointing ahead.

Molly could see it, still sitting near the volcano wall. There was a great hole in the middle of the floor where the ground had simply melted away. Lava boiled and churned there, and the two friends eased their bubble around the edge of it towards the creamy-pink slice of the magical conch.

"Oh – but how do we get your shell *inside* the bubble?" Molly wondered, suddenly realizing the drawback of being in a sealed space. They couldn't reach out and grab it – the shimmering golden wall was between them!

A few centimetres away, Pearl's shell was glowing brightly – and now Molly's shell shone with light too. All of a sudden, it began to pull against Molly's necklace, as if it was being drawn towards Pearl's shell by a magnetic force. Just then, Pearl's piece of conch was caught by a jet of boiling water and whirled straight up, even closer to the other side of the bubble wall.

On impulse, Molly grabbed her conch and pressed it against the inside of the bubble... There was another flash of golden light and the surface of the bubble sparkled all over. Molly blinked at the brightness – and then, when she looked again, there were *two* pieces of shell inside the bubble!

"Fantastic!" she cried joyfully, passing Pearl's shell to her. "Conch magic is so amazing." She could dimly hear the volcano rumbling again, although the bubble seemed to be blocking out most of the sounds from outside, as well as the fiery heat.

Pearl threw her arms around Molly. "Brilliant!" she cried. "Oh, I can't believe it! I'm so happy!" She stroked her shell lovingly. "And now that I've got this, I can make—"

She stopped speaking as another gigantic rumble thundered through the volcano – loud even inside the bubble.

"Uh-oh," said Molly in alarm. "Too late!"

"Hold tight," Pearl said, grabbing Molly. "Let's hope this bubble is strong enough because I think she's going to—"

WHOOSH!

"—blow!" screamed Pearl.

"Whoa-oh-oh!" Molly yelled as
the bubble was buffeted up the volcano on
a torrent of boiling lava. It was like the wildest
roller coaster ever – the scariest, fastest ride of
her life. "Whoa-oh-oh!" she screamed again,
as the bubble soared from the top of the
volcano. She just caught a glimpse of the
mass of sea snakes being showered
far and wide, spraying from Crater
Mountain in all directions.

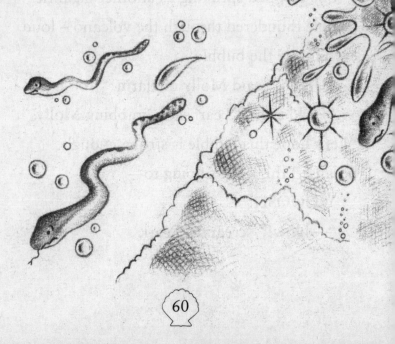

Lava was splurging out behind them, its red molten form turning grey and rocky within moments of entering the cool ocean water outside the mountain.

And then the bubble was tossed right out of the sea on a jet of steam, and Molly and Pearl could only stare white-faced at one another as they were sent sailing through the air...

Chapter Five

SPLASH! The bubble plunged back down into the sea once more, a safe distance from the volcano. As it broke the surface of the water, the golden walls of the bubble dissolved and vanished from sight. Everything became suddenly louder and brighter, and it felt, for a moment, as if the sea was roaring in Molly's ears.

Adrenalin surged around her body and she found she couldn't stop laughing in nervous relief. "Oh wow!" she cried. "That was so amazing! Can you believe we've just been shot out of a volcano?"

Pearl was laughing too, and flung her arms around Molly. "Thank goodness the magic helped us," she said. "And now I've got my conch piece back, the volcanoes should all be much calmer. I can't wait to tell the Merqueen!" As she was speaking, her shell was shooting out emerald-green sparkles of light through the water, and Molly knew that it was working its special deep-sea magic.

Molly beamed. "Let's get back to the Undersea Kingdom, then," she said, "before the Dark Queen discovers her sea snakes failed in their mission, and sends them after us."

Pearl glanced around quickly, but there was no sign of the snakes. "You're right, we should hurry away," she agreed. "Carlotta won't be at all happy to hear her army have missed their chance to get another piece of the conch. Besides, I'm so looking forward to telling Queen Luna and the Shell-Keepers our great news. Only one piece of the conch left to find now!"

Pearl slipped her shell into a small green bag that she wore, and then the two mermaids set off together, both feeling jubilant at what had happened. Molly kept replaying the volcano's eruption over and over in her head, still not quite able to believe that she and Pearl had survived such a dramatic experience. Whatever would her parents say if she dropped into conversation the fact that she'd been shot out of the biggest deep-sea volcano in a magical bubble? She had to bite back a giggle at the thought of their faces. Of course, she *wouldn't* say any such thing – not to anyone! – but it really was quite a story...

She was so lost in her thoughts that she was startled to hear a voice nearby. "Pearl! Molly! What news?"

Molly slowed to a halt and stared around, as did Pearl.

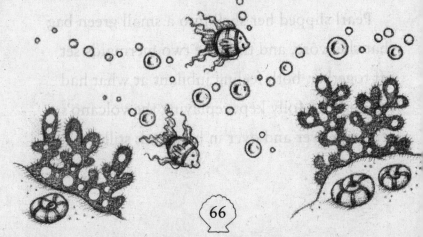

"Princess Silva!" Pearl said in surprise, as the Merqueen's daughter approached. "What are you doing here?"

The princess seemed a bit agitated, Molly thought, and her eyes were bloodshot and red. Had she been crying? But she was smiling now as she swam towards them, her purple cloak rippling behind her in the water.

"Pearl, is it true you've got your piece of the conch?" she called.

"Yes!" Pearl beamed. "I'm so happy. We were just on our way back to—"

The princess interrupted, her smile becoming wider. "That's wonderful news," she said. She licked her lips. "May I see it?"

Pearl looked a little surprised at the request, but bobbed a curtsy and drew her shell out from its place in her bag. "Of course, Your Highness," she said politely, holding it out on her palm. "Here."

Molly was just wondering *how* Princess Silva
had heard their news – had the story really got
round the ocean so quickly? – when all of a
sudden, she felt something brush
against her tail. She looked down
to see a black and yellow sea
snake glaring at her, its
eyes threatening, its
forked tongue poking out.

She yelped and darted out of the way quickly – and then saw a whole group of snakes behind that one, their tails rippling through the water as they approached. "The snakes are back!" she squealed in fright. "Let's get out of here!"

Everything happened very fast then. Pearl made to tuck her shell safely back into its bag, but before she could, Princess Silva suddenly thrust out a pale hand and snatched it from

Pearl's palm. Then she turned and darted away with it, swimming quickly into the distance.

"Wait for us!" Pearl yelled, grabbing Molly's hand and swimming after the princess.

Molly's head was reeling as she powered through the water with her friend. The snakes had appeared so suddenly, so silently, that they had caught the mermaids off guard. But why had Silva snatched Pearl's piece of the conch?

"I don't understand," Molly said breathlessly, as she and Pearl swam after the princess, who was racing ahead through the water. "Why did she take your shell?"

Pearl seemed baffled too. "I don't know," she said. "Maybe to keep it safe from the snakes? She must be terrified of them – look how fast she's going!"

Molly and Pearl followed the disappearing figure of the princess. "Your Highness! Princess Silva!" Pearl yelled after her, but the princess didn't turn her head or slow down for a moment.

Molly felt a growing sense of unease. This wasn't right. She wasn't convinced by Pearl's explanation at all. Before she could think about it any more though, a group of sea snakes swam smoothly in front of her and Pearl, cutting them off from the disappearing princess. Their red eyes flashed warningly, and their little forked tongues

flickered between their jaws. "Go away!" Pearl
cried, but the snakes merely reared their heads
at the mermaids, and surged towards them.

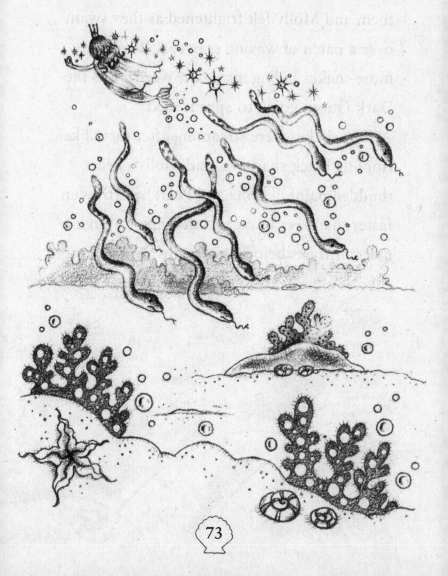

"This way!" Pearl yelled, grabbing Molly's hand and swerving beneath the snakes. They had to skim right along the seabed to avoid them and Molly felt frightened as they swam over a patch of waving seaweed. Were there more snakes hiding inside the weed? Was the Dark Queen going to appear next?

The snakes were streaming after them like rippling black shadows, and Molly's heart thudded painfully. She and Pearl had to swim faster than ever to escape, dodging through a maze of rocks before eventually losing them.

"Phew," Pearl said, panting. "I think we've thrown them off."

Molly looked around breathlessly. "I'm glad we've lost them," she said. "But I think we've lost the princess too – and your piece of the conch, Pearl!"

The mermaids scoured the sea in all directions for a sign of the princess's cape or a glimpse of her silvery crown, but could see no trace of her.

"I don't like this," Pearl said. "What if the Dark Queen has got her?" She gave a shout.

"Your Highness! Where are you?"

There was no reply. Then Molly thought she saw a flash of purple from within a hollow area of rock nearby. "I think the princess might be hiding in there," she whispered in astonishment, pointing to the rocks.

Pearl and Molly swam closer to investigate – and sure enough, tucked tightly into a small opening in the rocks was the princess herself.

She looked startled to see them. Her cheeks burned, and Molly had the distinct feeling she was about to dodge out from the

rocks and swim away from them again – but
Pearl took her by the wrist. "Your Highness –
are you all right? I thought the Dark Queen
might have got you – or the snakes. Did any
of them bite you? Are you okay?"

The princess seemed confused
and wouldn't look them in
the eye. "I'm fine," she
mumbled.

"It's just...well,
I wanted my shell
back," Pearl went
on. "I've only
just got it again,
so I really don't
want it out of my
sight. I was quite
surprised when you
swam off with it like that."

77

The princess still wasn't looking directly at Pearl, but pressed the piece of conch into Pearl's hand. "Sorry, I was just..." Her voice trailed away. "Sorry. Just trying to...protect it for you. Anyway, I'd better go. See you."

And with that, she was off, swimming away from them. As she went, Molly couldn't help noticing that her eyes still seemed to have a glimmer of red in them. Surely that didn't mean...

Molly shook herself. No! Princess Silva was the Merqueen's daughter, after all. It was crazy even to *think* that she might be working for the Dark Queen.

"That was strange," she commented to Pearl, watching the princess swim into the distance.

"Very," Pearl said thoughtfully. "I think we should follow her back to the Undersea Kingdom, just to make sure she's all right.

She was acting very oddly." She slipped her shell back into her drawstring bag, pulling the top tight. "I wonder what she's doing in this part of the ocean, anyway? I'm not sure Queen Luna would be very happy about her being so far from home."

Molly shrugged, her eyes still on Silva. Pearl seemed very trusting of the princess but she couldn't help feeling more doubtful. Before she could say anything though, Pearl pointed ahead. "Looks like I'll have to make the journey alone, Molly. Dawn is breaking – do you see the light shining?"

Molly let out a groan. Sure enough, a shaft

of bright morning sunlight was streaking through the water. She knew what that meant – her adventure was over, and it was time to return home. "But Pearl – will you be all right on your own?" she asked, feeling fearful for her new friend. What with the sea snakes and Princess Silva's peculiar behaviour, she knew *she* wouldn't have liked to swim all the way to the kingdom alone.

Pearl smiled. "Course I will," she said. "Molly – you've been fantastic. I'm so glad you're our secret mermaid." She hugged her. "See you soon, I hope. And thanks again!"

Molly hugged her back, but not for long. She could feel a new current tugging her upwards, and seconds later she was pulled out of Pearl's grasp, and sent spinning up through the water, with a whirl of bubbles all around her.

Chapter Six

Molly knew before she opened her eyes that she was back in bed, and the adventure was over. She buried her face in the pillow, not wanting it to end quite yet, wishing she could have stayed a mermaid just long enough to have made sure of Pearl's safe return to the Undersea Kingdom...

It was silly of her, really – after all, Pearl was perfectly able to look after herself; it

wasn't as if she needed Molly to hold her hand
– absolutely not! Yet it had been such a strange
and unusual visit to the ocean this time,
especially with the peculiar behaviour of
Princess Silva right at the end. It wasn't as if it
was the first time she'd noticed the princess
behaving oddly either – there had been other
instances too. When she'd helped Coral find her
piece of conch in the tropical reef, Molly had
thought she'd seen Princess Silva there, in the
distance. And hadn't Delphi said something
about Princess Silva hanging around, too?
Something didn't quite add up.

She yawned and stretched, pushing her feet
right down to the end of the bed and then
wiggling her toes. It was funny to feel them
there again, after another adventure with her
powerful mermaid tail.

She stretched her arms above her head and as

she did so, she became aware that there was something in one of her hands. Opening her eyes at last and shuffling into a sitting position in bed, she uncurled her fingers and saw a milky-white pearl in her palm. A pearl from Pearl!

She smiled at the thought, and as her new friend's face drifted into her mind, Molly was sure she heard a faint, whispery voice calling from the ocean. *Molly...Molly...Molly...*

The voice faded away and Molly felt shivery, despite the warmth of her bedroom. "Thank you," she whispered into the silence, before setting her pearl down carefully on her bedside table next to the conch necklace. Then she swung her legs out of bed and went to open the curtains, bright sunlight falling into the bedroom as she did so. The light glinted on the silver padlock that kept her diary safe from prying eyes and her gaze lingered on the book of secrets for a few moments. She would *definitely* have to write up all her news in there soon. So much had happened to her since her family had moved to the bay!

"I just hope there'll be a happy ending to write in as well, though," she murmured aloud. She gazed down at the band of sparkling blue sea below, wondering when she'd have her next mermaid adventure. How she hoped she could help find the last piece of the conch before the Dark Queen! She shuddered, remembering the beady red eyes of the sea snakes and the way they'd given chase to her and Pearl. Whatever happened, she'd have to try her best for the mermaids. Even if it meant facing the Dark Queen herself...

"I guess I'll find out soon," she said, feeling both excited and scared at the idea. With one last look at the sea, she turned away and went downstairs for breakfast.

The End

Read on for a sneak
preview of Molly's next
magical underwater
adventure...

Return of the Dark Queen

Molly opened her eyes. Yes – she was underwater, and there was her beautiful green mermaid tail in the place where her legs had been! She gave it a flick and surged through the sea, smiling with happiness as her hair streamed out behind her. Oh, it was wonderful to be back in the Undersea Kingdom!

She looked about expectantly. Every time she'd become a mermaid so far, she'd appeared near one of the Shell-Keeper mermaids. This time, however, there was no one in sight. The water was a clear blue, and very cold, and the light seemed strange and eerie, filtering down dimly in shafts at intervals. Then she looked up and gasped. There was a ceiling of thick ribbed ice above her head! Was she in the Arctic Sea? Or maybe the Antarctic?

"Shivana?" she called hesitantly. The icy seas were where Shivana lived. There was no sign of the red-haired mermaid, though, just a shoal of silvery fish and a fat cinnamon-coloured walrus swimming some distance away, its stout flippers sending it along at a surprising speed. Molly watched it curiously as it swam to an open section of sea where the sunlight fell in, then heaved itself out of the water. She gazed down at the seabed and saw rocks and bare sand beneath her. Was it too cold even for seaweed to grow here?

"I guess I'd better explore," she said to herself after a few moments. Her magical shell must have brought her to this place for a reason, she decided, setting off through the water. Maybe she'd find Shivana's piece of the conch shell all on her own. Or maybe…

Molly froze as a sound reached her ears. A faint, muffled sound – rather like a cry. "Shivana?" she called out, louder this time. She swam in the direction of the voice. "Shivana, is that you?"

The voice was more distinct this time, and Molly's blood ran cold as she realized what was being shouted.

"Help! Somebody help me!"

Molly pushed hard with her tail fin to send herself shooting through the chilly sea at top speed. She moved out from under the ice ceiling to a lighter, warmer patch of water, where lumps of ice shifted and bobbed about above her head. Who was shouting for help? Was it Shivana? She couldn't see any sight of her mermaid friend, despite looking frantically in all directions.

"Where are you?" she called helplessly, searching everywhere as she swam. She was in a deeper area of water now, with lots of dark shadowy rocks below her.

"Here! In this cave!" the voice came again. "Molly – is that you?"

"Yes!" Molly replied, swimming towards the voice. A cave? She couldn't see any cave. "But I can't—" She broke off as she spotted a dark opening in the rocks nearby. She drew closer and saw that the opening became wider and deeper and that, yes, there *was* a rocky chamber within. But a gate made of long icicles, like bars, prevented her from going any further inside it.

To Molly's horror, Shivana was trapped behind the icicles like a prisoner!

To find out what happens next, read

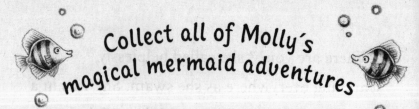

Collect all of Molly's magical mermaid adventures

Enchanted Shell 9780746096154

Molly is transported to the Undersea Kingdom for the first time, where she discovers she is the secret mermaid!

Seaside Adventure 9780746096161

To help Ella recover her piece of the magical conch, Molly must find a way to trap an angry killer whale.

Underwater Magic 9780746096178

Can Molly find some pirate treasure to win back Delphi's shell from a grumpy sea urchin?

Reef Rescue 9780746096192

Molly must help Coral find her shell to restore the ocean reefs, but a swarm of jellyfish stands in their way...

Deep Trouble 9780746096185

Pearl's conch piece is trapped in an undersea volcano and guarded by sea snakes. How can she and Molly release it?

Return of the Dark Queen 9780746096208

Molly must save Shivana from an Arctic prison before the Shell-Keeper mermaids can finally face the Dark Queen and complete the magical conch.

Seahorse SOS ⊚ 9781409506324

There's more trouble in the Undersea Kingdom and Molly joins in the search for the missing seahorses.

Dolphin Danger ⊚ 9781409506331

Molly and Aisha can hear faint calls for help but the dolphins are nowhere to be seen. Where can they be?

Penguin Peril ⊚ 9781409506348

Could the Dark Queen be behind the mysterious disappearance of the penguins from the icy seas?

Turtle Trouble ⊚ 9781409506355

There are some scary monsters lurking in the coral reef and they're guarding the turtles Molly has come to set free!

Whale Rescue ⊚ 9781409506393

Molly must not only save the trapped whales but also her mermaid friend, Leila.

The Dark Queen's Revenge ⊚ 9781409506409

The Dark Queen is back and she wants to rule the Undersea Kingdom with her bad magic. Can Molly put an end to her vile plans?

To find out more
about Molly and all her
mermaid friends, and have
some magical ocean fun,
check out
www.thesecretmermaid.co.uk